The HOUSE on Phantom Trail

BY STEPHEN PEREZ

ISBN: 978-1-965679-13-5 (sc)
ISBN: 978-1-965679-14-2 (e)

Rev. date: 09/26/2024

After the owner's pass,

the house comes alive...

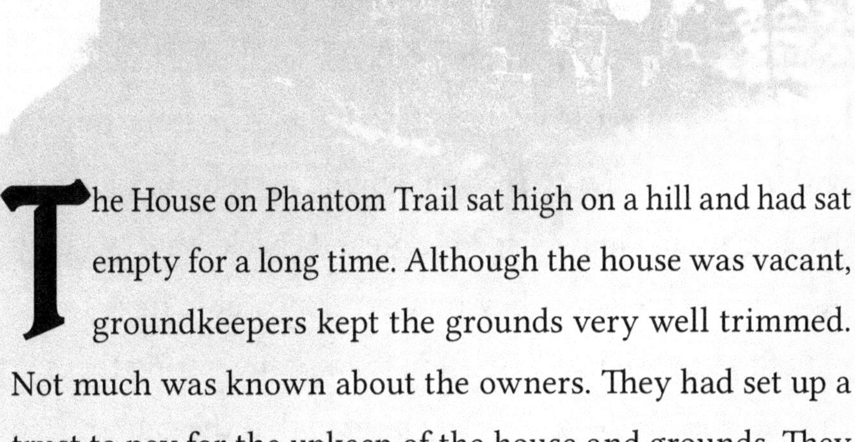

The House on Phantom Trail sat high on a hill and had sat empty for a long time. Although the house was vacant, groundkeepers kept the grounds very well trimmed. Not much was known about the owners. They had set up a trust to pay for the upkeep of the house and grounds. They were said to have been an elderly couple from Austria.

They hadn't had any children or family to speak of. After their passing, the house seemed to come alive. It was said to have special powers. There was a sign at the front door that read, ENTER AT YOUR OWN RISK. The caretakers did not know where it had come from, or who had put it up. The people of the town began to talk and wonder about all the goings-on at this house. Some said they heard strange noises coming from the house at all hours of the night. Others even said they had seen people going into the house, mostly at night.

The lights in the house would come on and go off like the house was lived in. The people started getting suspicious and scared. These events went on for some time. Since the house sat off by itself, the police thought that maybe it was just kids messing around. They told the people that they would keep an eye on it and respond accordingly. After that, things kind of settled down for a while. A month went by with no new activity. Then one night, a group of kids was driving around and decided to go and check it out. As they drove up to the gate, they thought they would have to get out of the car and walk in from there. After sitting there at the gate for a little while, they noticed that the gate started to open. They were apprehensive at first but decided that their curiosity was stronger than their fear. They drove in and went up the driveway. As they drove up to the house, they could see a light go on and then off inside the house. They parked the car and three boys, and one girl got out. They stood there in silence for what seemed like an eternity. As they walked up the stairs to the front door, something felt funny. Like they had just walked through a time portal.

When they got to the front door, one of the boys decided to ring the doorbell.

To their surprise, an older man opened the door. He said, "Won't you come in?" "We have been expecting you." The kids got scared and turned around like they were leaving. Before they could take another step, the man spoke up, "Don't be afraid. There is nothing to fear. Come in and I will explain everything." The kids were still a little apprehensive, but decided to go on in. One boy spoke up for the group, "My name is John. This is my sister, Ava. And these are our friends, Billy and David. What did you mean when you said that you were expecting us?" First, the old man said, "my name is Paul, and I am the keeper of this house. There are a few other people here that take care of different chores in this house. We have been expecting someone from the town to give us a visit." They were in a room that looked like a doctor's waiting room. Paul told the visitors to have a seat and he would explain everything about the house. He started by telling them a little bit about the old couple that had owned the house. "Their names were Gunter and Emily Strauss. They were an old Jewish couple that had survived the Holocaust. They were from a very wealthy old family. They had escaped and found their way to America where they kept a very low profile. I met them soon after they got here. We became very good friends, and we were inseparable until their death."

"On their deathbed, they asked me to hire some more people to help me look after this house. This house has some very special powers that were discovered after moving in." The kids seemed very interested to know about the powers of the house. Paul told them, "I will tell you all about the house, but first, you have to understand something." He told them, "Before you leave to go home, each one will be given a pill that will interact with that feeling you had when you walked up to the door. It is a security mechanism so that you will not remember anything about your experience here in this house."

"That said, each of you will go into a different room. The room works off of your memories. Whatever memory you think of the room will bring that memory to life. WARNING! So, make sure to think happy thoughts. Any bad memories will come to life as well." The kids were anxious to try out the rooms. John was the oldest, so he decided he would go first. He told the others, "Let me go first and wait until I come out before you guys try it." Paul let John into the room and told him to sit on the couch, the only furniture in the room. He asked John if he had a special memory that he would like to bring to life. John thought for a little while and then nodded his head. Paul told him to concentrate on that one memory and wait. John closed his eyes as Paul left the room. The door opened again and John thought that Paul had forgotten something. As John opened his eyes to ask what Paul had forgotten, he got the surprise of his life! The person that came walking through the door was not Paul, but rather John's father, who had passed away a few years earlier. His father, Henry, walked through the door and told John, "Wake up, you're going to be late for work. I must go pick up your mother from the salon, so I will take you to work." First, John was so engrossed in the memory that he did not remember anything else. What seemed like two years later, they were celebrating his father's birthday. They were doing a lot of running around and John got tired, so he sat on the couch to take a little nap. He heard a door open, and when he opened his eyes, he was back in the room. Paul was walking back in. John told Paul; "I was just with my dad. It was his birthday. It felt so real!" Paul reminded him about the special powers of the house. After that, John went back out to the lobby to see his friends. He asked them, "have y'all been here all this time?" They said yes that he had only been in there 30 minutes. John told them," I could have sworn I was gone for two years." John told Ava about their father and how real it had felt. Ava got excited and told Paul that she wanted to go next. Paul agreed but reminded Ava to think happy thoughts. He took her into the room and told her to sit on the couch and close her eyes. He brought her a drink just as he had done for John and told her, "In case you get thirsty." Paul left the room just as Ava closed her eyes. Something startled her and she opened her eyes. She was in the room that was hers when she was young!

Her mother was calling her from downstairs, saying supper was ready. She got up and went downstairs. Her mother told her that John was working late so he would not be eating supper with them. Dad was already seated at the head of the table. He smiled and asked how her day had been. She said it had been fine. Mother sat down and they ate supper in silence. The next day she woke up and went downstairs. Mom asked Ava if she wanted to go shopping. Ava said yes, so she went back upstairs to get dressed. Dad decided to stay home and just let the women go. Mom told Ava, "Okay, then we will just take all day and make it a girls' day out." They left and were gone all day. When they got home, it was late, and Dad had supper already waiting for them.

That night they stayed up late talking and laughing. It was a great night. When she woke up in the morning, it was John's graduation day. Three years before their dad passed, the day started with breakfast and got hectic after that. Mom told Ava they had a million things to do so they needed to get moving. They walked out the door and that day was a blur. That night, Ava went out with some of her friends to celebrate their graduations. When she got home later that night, she found John sitting on the porch in the dark. She asked him why he was sitting there. That is when John told her that their father was in the hospital. Ava asked about their mother and John told her that she was spending the night at the hospital with their father. They did not know what was wrong. And hopefully they would find out in the morning. During all of this, Paul had come into the room to check on Ava. He waited for a few minutes and then tried to wake Ava up, but she did not respond. Paul went out to the lobby to talk to John. He said, "She's not waking up. But don't worry. This has happened before." He explained to John, "Sometimes the person gets so deep into their memories, that they cannot come out. We will wait a little while and you can come with me, and we will try again."

Back to the memory, Ava was waking up the next day and her and John were driving to the hospital. Their mother was waiting outside for them and took them directly to the hospital chapel.

She explained to them, "the doctors have found cancer." At this news, Ava broke down. Their next year was spent in and out of hospitals, but Ava never gave up hope. Ava and her dad had had a very special relationship. She had always been daddy's little girl. One night, her father sat her down to talk. He explained to her," I will be leaving soon, and you need to be strong for your brother and your mother." He told her that he would always be with her and that this was not goodbye. He told her that they needed to cherish the days that they had left and for her not to worry. She fell asleep that night feeling very content. And when she woke up the next morning, she was back in the room at the house on Phantom Hill and Paul and John were walking in. Ava got up and hugged John. John was concerned and asked Ava if she was all right.

He told her, "We were so worried!" and proceeded to tell her what had happened. Ava said that she was fine and had enjoyed going back into that memory; otherwise, her memory would not have been complete. They went back out to the waiting room with the others. Paul asked if either of the other two boys would like to go in. Billy was hesitant but decided to give it a try. Paul took him into the room and told him to sit on the couch. He explained the process to him and then left the room. Billy sat there waiting, when he noticed the drink that Paul had left. He picked it up and drank all of it. He was sitting there and started to get up, frustrated because nothing was happening. Finally, he lost patience, got up, and opened the door to the next room. When he walked in, he got a big surprise. A familar dog jumped up on him. "Get down, Tiger!" he yelled. Tiger was Billy's dog that he had gotten for his birthday when he was eight!

Deep in the memory, Billy took Tiger outside to play ball. They played outside all day and had the time of their lives.

The two went inside and fell asleep on the couch. Then things took a turn. Billy's subconscious had kicked in and he began thinking about the automobile accident that had taken Tiger's life. His memory took him back to the car where his mother was driving. He saw the truck come out of nowhere and smash into their car on the driver's side. Tiger loved going for rides and had been in the back seat. When the rear passenger door flew open, Tiger had fallen to his death. Back in the room at the Phantom Hill house, Billy was thrashing and yelling. Paul, from the room next door, heard the noise and ran in to see what the problem was. When he opened the door, he saw Billy on the floor thrashing around. He quickly called for assistance and several other people that worked at Phantom Hill walked in wearing jumpsuits.

They were medical personnel, and they immediately started working on Billy. They worked on him for quite a while. Finally, Billy opened his eyes. Billy could still remember the memory, and he began crying. The medics gave him a sedative and by the time John and the others were allowed in the room with Billy, he had calmed down. Paul apologized to the group and said, "That was very unfortunate. A bad memory must have slipped in there. This is why it is important to have happy thoughts. I think that must be all for today."

Paul was showing them to the door when John remembered the special pill that they were supposed to receive. Paul explained, "There was something was in each of your drinks that will take care of any memories that might have surfaced when you were in the room." John then said, "But David didn't get a drink, did he?" David answered, "Yes, I got one when Ava went in. Don't you remember? I was very thirsty."

"That's right," John said. "I had forgotten all about that." "You will remember coming into this house," said Paul. "But you will not remember anything else that happened while you were here." The kids thanked Paul, walked out to their car, and left. It was nice of Paul to tell them about the old couple that had owned the house. As they drove back to town, they seemed happy and content.

After the kids left, the two medics who had come to assist were looking uneasy. Paul reminded them that the kids would not remember anything that had transpired at the house. He told them that they would have to have thick skin if they wanted to continue to work there. "We will need to get ready for the next group. I don't know when they will be coming, but I can promise you that they will come." Halloween was right around the corner. The house and the grounds started to take on an eerie look. Paul called all the staff into the room for a meeting. Paul reminded them that the house would soon be very busy with activity. A lot of people in the town thought that the house was empty. They thought it was just an empty old, haunted house. He told the staff to expect everything and to be ready for anything. Just as predicted, two weeks before Halloween, a car drove up to the gate. As a man started to get out, the gate automatically opened. The man got back into his car and proceeded to drive up the driveway. He pulled up in front of the house. The driver stayed in the car while two young men and two young women got out. They started looking around the yard as if they were looking for something. Then, they started walking around to the rear of the house.

They kept looking around the grounds and at the house itself. They made their way around the other side of the house and finally went up onto the porch. They started looking in the windows and even tried the front door to see if it was locked. It was, so they tried the doorbell. To their surprise, the door opened and there stood Paul. "Can I help you?" asked Paul. The couple was more than a little startled. "We thought this house was empty!" said one of the men. "Hi, my name is Harry. These others are Tom, Nancy, and Faith, and we are from the local college." "How may I help you?" asked Paul again. "Well, as you know, Halloween is in a couple of weeks," Harry said. "We were hoping to have a fundraiser for our school choir. We looked all around town at empty houses that might help us with the fundraiser. Our goal is to fix up a haunted house and then charge an admission fee to raise money. We thought this house would be perfect!" "This is the best one that we have found yet," insisted Nancy. "But now we see this house is not empty."

Paul assured them the house was not empty and agreed they might be able to work something out. He asked them, "Did you feel something funny when you walked up the steps to the porch?" They all nodded their heads, agreeing that they had. Paul said, "This house is not your normal, typical house. It has special powers. I am not at liberty to explain those powers to you right now. But if you want, you can come back after Halloween, and I will explain it all to you. But, if we do this, it will be your group's responsibility to make sure that all the people that go into the house come out safely. The group is also responsible for any damage done and the cleanup afterwards. If you agree to those terms, I think we can work something out. Also, if you notice anyone that gets a queasy feeling after walking up the steps, they will not be allowed to go into the house. They will be too sensitive to the powers of this house and if they are allowed to go in the house, they could get deathly ill."

"Again, it will be your responsibility to keep everyone safe." Harry and the group agreed to these terms and shook hands. "What about the staff you mentioned?" someone in the group asked. "Yes," said Paul, "they will be given a week off, except for Monroe, who will monitor the entrance." The kids understood and got ready to leave. Harry asked Paul if it would be okay to come up a week before Halloween to prepare. Paul said that would be fine. So, the kids got in the car and drove away.

Paul called another meeting with the staff to advise them of the plan. He told them they would all be given a week off when the kids came back to prepare. He told them that only one person would stay behind to monitor the entrance and keep everyone safe. He told all the others not to come back until a few days after Halloween. Paul was also planning to stay in the house.

Finally, the day came for the kids to show up. Just like clockwork, the gate opened for them, and they made their way up to the house. This group was a little bigger than the first time and they came in trucks. Paul met them at the door and told them that he would be in the house, but that he would try to stay out of their way and keep out of sight.

He reminded Harry of the terms and conditions and gave him the keys to the house. The trucks were full of supplies, which they started to unload. Right at the start, one of the men walked up the steps to the house and began to feel ill. Monroe, the door monitor, was there and told the man that he would not be able to participate. The man did not receive this well and proceeded to get loud and became irate when he was told he had to leave.

Harry came running up to intervene. He reminded the man of the terms and let him know that Monroe was just doing his job. He would have to go home. The man reluctantly left. Luckily, they did not have any more issues for the rest of the day. It was starting to get dark when Paul told Harry that they would have to call it a day.

The next day the group came a little earlier and got to work very fast. Harry asked Paul if it would be all right to work late into the night so that they could finish. Paul said it would be okay if not too late. And a little after 10 o'clock p.m., they finished. Harry told Paul that they wished they could have a night to do a practice run. Paul said again that he thought that would be okay.

The next day the group waited till it was almost dark to show up. Some of the young men got into positions to man their stations. They had Frankenstein, Dracula, and zombies placed in different areas. As kids walked through these areas, they planned to have spooky music playing in the background. They did a few practices runs and had a blast. Harry told Paul that they were satisfied, and that they would be leaving. Halloween was still a few days away, and Harry told Paul that they would not be back until Halloween Day. He mentioned that they would come a little early to make sure everything was ready to go.

Halloween came, and the group showed up to get everything set up. They had put flyers all over town, reminding people about the haunted house event.

As the sun was going down, people began showing up. They were even lined up outside of the gate! When it was just right, Harry gave Paul the signal to open the gate. The people started pouring in. They were told to keep their groups small, only three to four at a time. Just as promised, Monroe sat at the entrance of the house, out of the way, but cautiously observing all the people coming in. Every now and then, a person would walk up the steps and immediately seem disoriented. Monroe would take that person aside and explain that they would not be allowed in the house. He explained that it was for their own good.

A few hours later, they had a group come in from a neighboring town. As they walked up the steps, Monroe noticed one man that looked like he was becoming disoriented. They took him aside and explained that he also would not be allowed to participate. The man started yelling and got upset and became hostile. It took quite a few men just to get him settled down. And after he settled down, he was told to leave, or they would be forced to call the authorities. The man finally left, but he was not happy. The night ended without any more instances. Harry apologized to Paul and told him that they would be back to clean up the next day.

As promised, the following day the group showed up around lunchtime. They worked hard and fast to get everything cleaned up and back into place and were done before the sun went down. Before they left again, Harry asked Paul if it would be okay to come back the next week to learn more about the house. Paul told Harry that it had been a wild night and so maybe he should give it a couple of weeks before coming back. Harry understood and made plans to return after a couple of weeks had passed. Two days later, the Phantom Hill staff started to come back, and Paul called another meeting. He let the staff know that Harry and a group would be back. He did not know how big the group would be, and he encouraged them to be ready for anything.

Two weeks went by, and no one came around. On the third week after the Halloween event at Phantom Hill, a car came pulling up the driveway. The gate opened and the car drove up to the house. Sure enough, it was Harry and a few other people. They walked up the steps and Paul met them at the door. "I did not know if you and the group were coming. It has been a while," said Paul. "With the holidays, school and all our tests, we've been busy," replied Harry. "We really don't have a lot of time now either, but we were so curious about this house. We just had to come." Paul invited them in and told them to sit down. Paul invited them in and told them to sit down. Harry, one girl, and three other boys walked in and sat down on the couch. Paul started explaining about the house and the powers that it had. He explained all about the owners and the staff. A couple of the boys started laughing in disbelief. Paul told them that what he was saying was the truth, and that they could try it out if they wanted to. He went on to explain about the precautions and the pill that they would have to take. One of the boys volunteered to be the first to try it. So, Paul led him into a room and told him to sit down on the couch. He told him to concentrate on a memory that he would like to revisit and cautioned him to remember that it needed to be a happy memory. He put a drink on the table and left. The boy attempted to think of a happy memory that he would like to revisit. After sitting there for a while, he found that he could not come up with anything. He started to get frustrated and decided that he was right. It was all just a joke. This house did not have any powers. It was just a typical house! He was fuming and started to get up to leave. When he opened the door, he was suddenly at a football game, a high school football game. He was returning to his seat and sitting next to a girl that he had met two months before. He sat there cheering and watching the game for the rest of the night. After the game, he asked the girl if she was hungry. The girl said yes, so they decided to go meet some of their friends for a hamburger. They went to a hamburger joint nearby, and as they were sitting there eating and talking with friends, a few people from the other team walked in. They came across as somewhat belligerent when they started making accusations about how they believed they were cheated.

A boy named Sam and his friends argued back about how they had won, fair and square. As the two groups got louder, the workers at the hamburger joint had to ask them all to leave. Outside, the two groups got even louder and became hostile. Two of the boys started fighting. Sam did not like this, so he tried to break them up. It was all too much, and somehow Sam got punched and knocked out. When he came to, his jaw really hurt, but he was back in the room at Phantom Hill. He went back to the lobby where the others were waiting. He told them what had happened and how it felt so real! Another boy insisted that he was going next, but the one lone girl in the group asked if she could go next. Always a gentleman, Paul said that would be fine, and he led the girl into the room. He explained everything to her and was about to walk out when he noticed a drink on the floor next to the couch. He picked it up and walked out. In the other room, he asked the boy that had just come out if he was thirsty and reminded him that he should drink something after going through what he had just gone through. The boy agreed and said yes, he was thirsty, and then he took the drink from Paul and drank it. In the room, the girl was settling in, but was having trouble deciding on a memory. Suddenly, she heard a knock on the door. When she opened the door, her mother was standing there. ""Are you ready?"

" her mother asked. "We are going up to the cabin." While her mother was driving, the girl in the passenger seat opened the car window. She can feel the cool wind blowing in her face. When they get there, she sees her father and brothers were already there. It was late in the afternoon, and the girl said that she wanted to go swimming. The father said it was okay, but for the boys to go with her. He said that he would get the barbecue pit going so everything would be ready when they got out. In the meantime, mother was inside getting everything ready. When they were done, the kids got out of the lake and headed for the cabin. Dad was just finishing up and told the kids to get dried off and ready to eat. He told them he had a surprise for them. As they were sitting and eating, they heard a car drive up. Dad went out to greet the company. When he walked back into the cabin, there was a man with him, and he was carrying a guitar. Dad introduced him as an old family friend and said that he was a very well-known musician. He had called him and asked him to join them and be their entertainment. The man joined them at the table. When they were done, they all headed outside. The man got his guitar and started playing for them. He had been playing for a little while when he decided to play a very slow and soft tune. The soft tune caused the girl to just doze off.

She woke up to someone tapping on her shoulder. Paul had come in to wake her up." I was getting worried about you," Paul said. "You have been out for over an hour." The girl smiled at Paul and said, "That was the best!" They both walked back out to the main room, and Paul told them that it was getting late and that they should be on their way. The other boys were feeling left out and spoke up about that. Paul apologized and told them that the house would be closing for the holidays, but that they could come back after the first of the year. The boys did not like it but had no other options. They were expecting a harsh winter, and Paul told them he would put up a sign when he was ready to reopen. The group got in their car and drove away.

It *was* a very harsh winter, as had been predicted. January came and went with no movement. By late February, Paul decided that it was time to open again. He went out to the gate and put up the open sign. Early March, and still no one had come to the house on Phantom Hill. Paul had told the staff to be ready for anything. Paul started noticing a difference in the house, and he asked the staff if they noticed it as well. The staff agreed that something seemed off but said that they could not put a finger on it. There were subtle things. Furniture moved a certain way. Small items went missing completely. Paul was not sure if it meant anything. He did not totally know everything about the house. The old couple had mentioned the name and number of a person that might be able to help, so Paul decided to hold off on opening the house. He walked out to the gate to take down the open sign, and as he was doing so, a truck pulled up and a man got out. "Sorry," said Paul, "we are not quite ready to open yet." The old man walked up to Paul and introduced himself. "I believe the owners of this house gave you my name and number. My name is Bruno, Bruno Wagner. I have a history with this house." "You know about the powers of this house?" asked Paul. "Yes, I do," answered the man, "and I am here because I sensed that there was something wrong."

"Yes, there is something wrong," answered Paul. "We experienced a very harsh winter, and afterwards, we noticed little things, like items being moved and other items just gone completely." "I will need at least a week to investigate and see what is wrong. Will that be a problem?" asked Bruno. "That will not be a problem," " answered Paul. "We will fix up a room so you can stay here on the grounds." For the next two weeks, Bruno took his time wandering around and inspecting things inside and outside of the home. After the two weeks, he met with Paul and all the staff. "After being inside and outside of the house, I have come to a conclusion." "With all the weather and as harsh as the winter was this year," said Bruno, "I believe that the time portal has been damaged. I don't know how severe that damage is currently." Paul asked him if it would be okay to open the house again to the public. "I think that would be okay," answered Bruno. "I will stay on a while longer just to see how things go." So, it was decided, and Paul walked over to the gate and put the open sign back out again. Two months went by with no activity. Paul started to get worried. He decided to go out and put up a bigger open sign. He put it up and turned around to go back to the house when he noticed that the house had a certain glow about it. He went back to the house and asked Bruno to walk out to the gate with him. They got to the gate and Paul told Bruno, "Now turn around and look at this house." "I don't like it. I don't like this one bit," said Bruno.

"You will need to take down that open sign again. Take it down until further notice," Bruno told Paul. And so, Paul took down the sign again, and they both walked back to the house. "I have a team of experts that I put together for situations such as this one," said Bruno. "I was hoping that I would not need them, but it looks like I will have to call them." "How long do you think this will take?" asked Paul.

"I don't know,"" answered Bruno. "It could take a long time."
To save on expenses, Paul decided to let the staff go for now.
"I will call you when things are back up," Paul informed them.
Two days later, a van with ten passengers drove up to the
gate. Bruno went out to greet them. He invited them all in,
so they could have a meeting. He explained everything to
them. "You all have a different line of expertise," said Bruno.
"So, with that, I want you all to walk around the house and
all over the grounds and tell me what you see and what you
think." The team of people did just that. They walked in and
around the house, and they walked around the grounds. For
two weeks they did this. After that time, they asked to have
a meeting with Bruno and Paul. They surmised that there
in fact was a problem, but not one that couldn't be fixed.
They asked Paul if it would be possible for them to have
the house to themselves for a month. With everyone gone,
even Paul himself, Paul did not like the idea, but thought
to himself that there was no other solution. They told him
they would need volunteers but would take care of that.
Paul hesitantly agreed and got ready to leave. The next day,
Paul gave Bruno the keys to the house and left. As he was
driving off, he looked back and noticed that the glow had
gotten brighter. He just shook his head and kept driving.
Back at the house, Bruno and the team got to work. We will

need to go into town and get some volunteers, stated one of the men. Bruno did not like this either but knew that there was no other way. A couple of men jumped in the van and headed to town. They were looking for homeless people, men or women, it didn't matter. They would explain what they wanted and then offer them money. As they were driving around, they came upon a couple of prospects. They pulled over and talked to the two men. They explained what they wanted and told them that they could expect to be paid for the mission. They also advised them of the risks involved and that they could not guarantee their safety. They would have to sign a release form. The two men agreed, got in the van, and began the drive back to the house. On the way back, they saw another man walking down the street.

They made this man the same offer, and he readily accepted. When they got to the house, all the men got out of the van and walked towards the house. When they got to the front door, one of the men became disoriented almost immediately and started acting funny. They quickly took him aside and told him that they would not be able to use him as part of the project. As they walked him back to the van, they told him that they would pay him anyway. They gave him some money, thanked him, and drove him back to town. When they returned to the house, they started the process with the other two men. They took one man into the room and explained everything to him. As they left the room, they left a drink on the floor by the couch. The man sat on the couch and started thinking of some memories. He heard a knock on the door, so he got up to answer it. He got the biggest surprise of his life, because when he answered, his wife was on the other side. She asked him, "Are you ready?" He answered, "Ready for what?" His wife just laughed and said, "We're going to meet John and Alice for supper." "Did you forget again, you silly?" John had been his friend since childhood. He got his coat and followed her out of the house and when they got to the restaurant, John and Alice were already there waiting for them. After supper, they went bowling and they had the best time. When they returned home, they got ready for bed. He heard the doorbell and went to answer it. He could not imagine who it could be at that hour of the night. When he answered the door, he was back in the house on Phantom Hill. The others asked him how everything had gone. He started crying and said that everything had gone fine. He thanked them for getting the opportunity to see his wife once again. He said everything felt so real. They reminded him not to forget the drink that was left for him.

He drank it quickly and went to sit down in the lobby. Everyone was talking about how easy everything had gone for the trial. "I don't like it," said one man. "It was too easy. It's like the house is trying to trick us into thinking everything is okay. We need to do some more trials to make sure." This time they brought a woman in. They sat her down and explained everything to her. After talking to her for a while, they left a drink on the floor and walked out. The first thing she did was drink the drink. She was so thirsty. She started thinking about her husband and the next thing she knew; she was in the house that she had lived in years before. It was midday and she was watching a show on TV. She was thinking to herself, I better get started on supper. She made her way into the kitchen and was about to start supper when the phone rang. She went to answer it and when she picked it up, it kind of shocked her and sounded funny. It was the police on the other end. They asked her what her husband's name was. She answered and they told her that she needed to come down to the police station immediately. She asked the police what was going on and they told her they would not tell her over the phone. When she got to the police station, she walked in and up to the counter. "Hello," she said. "My name is Matilda. Y'all called me about my husband, Tom." "Let me find out," said the person behind the counter. They went into a back room and were gone for a few minutes. They came back and told her that there must be some mistake. No one from there had called her. Matilda told them someone called her saying they were the police and that she needed to come to the police station. "I'm sorry, ma'am," said the police officer, "but we do not have any record of this. I think someone is playing games with you, Matilda." Matilda felt very confused and left and went back home. She had been home about 30 minutes when the phone rang again. She picked it up. The person on the other end said that they were the police again and that she needed to come down to the station. "Whoever this is," said Matilda, "you need to stop playing games! It is not funny!" "This is no game" said the person on the phone. "Your husband is in grave danger." "I was just at the police station," said Matilda. "They said that they had not called me. Who is this??" Click, the phone went dead. Just as Matilda hung up the phone, her husband walked in the door. She ran to him, crying and a bit hysterical. But, when she pulled away from him, she noticed it was not her husband.

She screamed at the person, "who are you?" Just as the man was going to answer, she fainted. When she woke up, she was back in the Phantom Hill House. She was crying uncontrollably. The people came in and tried to comfort her. "What happened?" they asked. "Well," she said, "I was thinking about my husband, and something took over. It was something I never went through. But it felt so real." "I'm sorry," said the technician. "It has something to do with this house." They took her out to the lobby. "There is a definite problem," said one technician. "We must keep testing until we find the glitch." They brought in one other person. He was an older man. They took him in, gave him the drink, and explained everything to him. "Do you have anything stronger?" asked the man. "You don't need anything stronger." answered the technician. As they left the room the man just sat there. After a few minutes, he fell asleep. He started dreaming about his life, and when he was in the war and how much he missed his wife. Then everything started getting blurry and dark. He tried to wake up, but he couldn't. It felt like he was falling deeper and deeper into the darkness. Still dreaming, he could see a flicker of light in the distance. As he walked toward it, the light got brighter and brighter. Not knowing where it went, he tried to stop himself, but the light kept pulling him in. The light got really bright, and then it was gone, and so was the man. From the other room, the technician saw a flash of light under the door. They went into the room to see what it was. The room was empty and there was no sign of the man. They called Fred, who was the head technician. "This is why we wanted to get homeless people. They will not be missed so much. There is definitely something wrong. We must figure out where the problem is. We will have to do it again; except this time we will take video."

"We will set up cameras at every angle so we can see where things are going wrong." "Let's use another female. It seems like this might be gender-driven." They brought in another woman, explained everything to her, and left the room. They had forgotten to leave a drink, so she went to the door and asked them for the drink. When she opened the door, she was in a bar, the bar where she had worked for years, where she had met her husband. This was not a good memory for her. She had no idea how she had wound up there. She had not been thinking about that memory. She tried hard to think about something else. She went back to when she was a little girl playing with her dolls, but a minute later she was back at that bar. A man was yelling at her and grabbing her. The woman kept trying to wake up to no avail. She noticed that all the people in the bar were faceless. The man kept tugging at her and would not let her go. She finally broke free and ran toward the door. When she opened the door, she was back in the Phantom Hill house. The technicians took her back into the room and sat her down on the couch. They explained to her that they had videotaped the whole incident. They asked her if she would sit and watch the video with them. She could take them through the events step by step. They wanted to know what was going through her head throughout the event. She told them it was wrong from the beginning. As soon as she opened the door, she told them that the memory was the furthest thing from her mind and that she did not even know how it had come up. As they watched the video, they noticed that when they came to the point when she opened the door, there was an eerie kind of mist that she walked through. As she went on, the mist was draped around her. The technicians were baffled. They did not understand how the house could bring out a memory from deep within her psyche, a memory that she had not even thought about. They asked her if she would mind going through the experience once again. This time, a technician would stay in the room with her, and they would videotape it once again. She agreed, and everyone took their positions. She started off thinking about her childhood and playing with dolls. The house kept trying to bring up other negative memories. Against her will, the house brought up the memory of her divorce. It had been a very messy divorce.

Her husband had been very abusive. He had not wanted to grant her the divorce.

As the memory went on, she began to mumble and thrash. Seeing this, the technician walked over to her and attempted to wake her up. As he was shaking her, there was a loud boom that blasted the technician backwards! The force blasted him across the room and slammed him against the wall. He was knocked out cold. Fred and the other technicians in the other room heard the boom and tried to enter the room. However, the door was locked. "The house has gotten out of control," said Fred. "What do we do now?" asked the technicians. "Send for Bruno," said Fred. Bruno had been sleeping in an upstairs bedroom. Back in the room, the woman was still thrashing around. She was remembering how her husband had made her life hard, how he vowed to leave her penniless. That is how she had come to be homeless. By this time, Bruno had made it down to the lobby. Fred explained everything to Bruno. Somehow, Bruno got the door open and attended to the woman. It took a little while, but they managed to wake the woman up. Some medics came in to attend to the technician that had been blasted. The woman was still very distraught and crying. "This is very serious," said Bruno. "I suggest that we close this house down. For now, until we find out what's going on, let these people go. No more tests." Fred agreed and went to give the woman the drink that they had forgotten to give her earlier. They waited for three hours and then loaded all the homeless volunteers into the van and took them back into town. Bruno said, "Fred, we need to call Paul back and tell him what we have found and what we are doing." Bruno told one of the other technicians to take care of that and they drove back to the house and waited for Paul. When Paul arrived, they took him into the lobby, sat him down, and told him all that they had done. They told him about the missing man and everything else that had gone on. Paul was very uneasy, to say the least. "What do we do now?" asked Paul. "I have talked to all of the technicians," said Bruno. "We all agreed that the house should be shut down. For now, anyways, we think that the house should be left completely alone for a couple of months. Then we come back and reinvestigate everything." Paul did not like this idea but thought it best. Bruno and his crew left but told Paul to call them when the time was right. Paul spent the night there that night. The next day, Paul turned everything off and double-checked everything. He drove out the gate, put a big "closed" sign up, and left. He left a note for the groundkeepers, saying that they would no longer be needed. The house sat like that for a couple of months. The grounds got so overgrown, and that made the house really looked deserted. One night, a truck pulled up to the gate with its lights turned off. A man got out and went to make sure that the house was empty. When he was satisfied that it was, he came back to the truck and unloaded a couple of big gas cans. The man's name was George. He was the man that had gotten thrown out of the house. He remembered just how he had been treated. He had not liked it and was still upset about it. He took the gas cans and snuck under the fence. He started pouring gas all around the house until both gas cans were empty. He lit a match and ignited the gas. He then went around it to the back of the house and did the same. He ran out to the truck and watched the house catch fire. "Last time you'll be treating me that way!" he said, as the house was engulfed and he walked away.

www.ingramcontent.com/pod-product-compliance
Lightning Source LLC
Chambersburg PA
CBHW070357310726
48977CB00002B/478